The Boy Who Held Back the Sea

The Boy Who Held Back the Sea

Paintings by THOMAS LOCKER

Retelling by Lenny Hort

DIAL BOOKS   NEW YORK

Published by Dial Books
A Division of NAL Penguin Inc.
2 Park Avenue : New York, New York 10016

Published simultaneously in Canada
by Fitzhenry & Whiteside Limited, Toronto
Text copyright © 1987 by Dial Books
Illustrations copyright © 1987 by Thomas Locker
All rights reserved
Printed in Hong Kong by South China Printing Co.
Designed by Jane Byers Bierhorst
First Edition
W
1 2 3 4 5 6 7 8 9 10

Library of Congress Cataloging-in-Publication Data

Hort, Lenny : The boy who held back the sea.

Adaptation of : Hans Brinker, or
The silver skates / Mary Mapes Dodge.
Summary : By blocking a leaking hole in the dike,
a young boy saves his town from destruction.
[1. Netherlands—Fiction.] I. Locker, Thomas, 1937— ill.
II. Dodge, Mary Mapes, 1830–1905. Hans Brinker,
or The silver skates. III. Title.
PZ7.H7918Bo 1987 [E] 86-32893
ISBN 0-8037-0406-2   ISBN 0-8037-0407-0 (lib. bdg.)

The art for each picture consists of an oil painting,
which is color-separated and reproduced in full color.

To Anthony
T. L.

For my parents
L. H.

Pieter had just been sent to his room and now there was a knock. He expected to see Papa, and maybe Papa's belt, but it was only Grandmother and the cat. "I thought a story might cheer you up," she said, and settled into a chair with Wilhelmina on her lap.

When I was your age, Grandmother began, a boy like you lived in this very town. His father was a brewer just like your father. Jan wasn't really a bad boy, but you couldn't call him a good boy either. He was always off hunting or gazing over the dike out to sea when he should have been studying. Worse, he was always running back into town trying to arouse the guard because he'd thought he'd seen enemy soldiers or sea serpents.

One Sunday morning Jan asked his mother if he might be excused from church. He had promised to go read to Mr. Schuyler, a blind miller who lived five miles up the canal. His mother blessed her son's good heart. She sent him off with a splendid lunch and Mr. Schuyler's favorite rhubarb pie. The boy's dog trotted along with him.

As soon as Jan was out of his mother's sight, he sat down under the king's statue and ate that pie himself. He took out his sling and sent a chunk of pie up into the statue's crown for the pigeons. A man saw him shoot a rock through the schoolhouse window, but it was only old Captain Blauvelt. Whether or not the stories that he was a pirate were true, he was surely the last man to report a troublemaker. Jan put the sling in his pocket and went off to the woods to hunt squirrels.

The boy didn't much care for the lunch his mother had worked so hard on. He gave most of it to the dog, then got a blazing fire going and roasted a squirrel he had killed.

After that feast and his day of mischief, the boy was tired. He walked over to the dike, where he could smell the salt sea air and dream of pirate ships. He lay down in a favorite spot and was surprised to feel a trickle of water running down his back. He looked closely and was startled to find that the mighty ocean was leaking through a small hole in the dike. Even a naughty boy like Jan knew that a small leak unchecked would get bigger and that if the dike should give way a terrible flood might drown the whole town.

He couldn't ignore that leak. Jan knew he'd be in trouble if his mother found out that he'd never gone to Mr. Schuyler's, but still he ran back to get help. He found the constable talking with the schoolmaster, and shouted that the dam was leaking. But the constable just told him to go back to watching for sea monsters and the schoolmaster said that lying boys who didn't go to church always came to bad ends. When Jan kept insisting that it was true, the constable finally sent him back to the dike and promised to bring help.

But when the boy and his dog got back to the dam, there was nobody following them. And the leak had gotten worse. The hole was still small, but the flow was more than a trickle now. Jan tried to pack in a handful of dirt, but a moment later it came spurting out. He wadded up his handkerchief and tried to make a plug out of that, but of course it gave way as soon as he let go. If he could only hold back the water for a few minutes until help came. . . . He wrapped the handkerchief around his finger and dug it into the tiny gap in the earthen wall. The sun was going down, but for now, at least, the flow had stopped.

Storm clouds were gathering and the evening was turning cold. Jan had given up on the constable and the schoolmaster, but he was sure that someone would come along. He remembered the stories he'd read of faithful dogs fetching help for their wounded masters, but he was glad that his dog was still at his side. The hand that held back the sea was numb, but the boy hugged the dog with his free arm. "Someone will come soon," he said, "and think what heroes we'll be." But he wasn't sure he believed it himself.

The boy heard thunder as he listened to the clock in the tower striking midnight. Then he heard footsteps. The dog growled as lightning lit up a face. It was Captain Blauvelt, and God only knows what wickedness that man was up to at such an hour. But he listened to the boy's story and ran off to get help.

The captain stumbled into town shouting for the guard. They appeared and arrested him for disorderly conduct. The constable suggested that perhaps this was the man who went around breaking glass while good people were in church. Jan's mother heard the noise and came to her window. She was angry that her son had spent the night out without permission, and she said a prayer that he wouldn't grow up to be like the man the night watch were leading away.

Then it was dawn and the storm was over. Jan was shivering and delirious when he heard the voice of the schoolmaster: "Bad boy to be out worrying your mother at such an hour…" Only slowly did the man realize why the boy was lying in such an awkward position. The boy himself was long past telling about it, but for a little while longer he stayed there as the schoolmaster at last brought men with tools. In time somebody did think to fetch Jan's mother and father, and it was they who finally wrapped a blanket around him and carried him home.

But at your age a child can survive most anything, and in a few days Jan was up and about again. The town held a great festival to honor the young hero who had saved everybody from the worst flood since Noah, but when it was time for the banquet, the boy was nowhere to be found. Jan had sneaked off to read to Mr. Schuyler and his housekeeper, and he'd even brought along a rhubarb pie.

The cat in Grandmother's lap was snoring now, but Pieter wasn't. "Come to the table now, darling?" the woman asked her grandson. When they rejoined the family, it was as if nothing wrong had ever happened. But Pieter could hardly wait for dinner to be over so he could go out to keep watch at the dike himself.